Catherine Marshall's

storybook for children

Catherine Marshall's

storybook for children

Edited by
David Hazard

Illustrated by
Joe Boddy

Published by
√ chosen books

FLEMING H. REVELL COMPANY
OLD TAPPAN, NEW JERSEY

Library of Congress Cataloging-in-Publication Data

Marshall, Catherine, 1914-1983
    Catherine Marshall's storybook for children.

    Summary: A collection of stories and poems illustrat-
ing Christian teachings about such things as faith,
humility, honesty, and kindness.
    1. Children's stories, American. |1. Conduct of life
—Fiction. 2. Christian life—Fiction. 3. Short stories|
I. Hazard, David. II. Boddy, Joe, ill. III. Title. IV. Title:
Storybook for children.
PZ7.M3557St 1987 |Fic| 87-8984
ISBN 0-8007-9109-6

A Chosen Book
Copyright © 1987 by Calen, Inc.

Chosen Books are published by
Fleming H. Revell Company
Old Tappan, New Jersey
Printed in the United States of America

Contents

Introduction 7
For a Spring Day 9
The Dog Who Had an Idea 10
Look for a Lovely Thing 14
The King Who Burned the Biscuits 15
God's Little Nightlights 20
The Boy on the Fence 21
Let's Play 26
Scary Things Around the Corner 27
Under God's Canopy 30
The Frog Who Flew 31
Do You Know Who Made You? 36
A Blackbird Never Forgets 37
My Pocket 42
Thorns and Roses 43
Thank You, Lord 46
Good-Night 48

Introduction

The world of childhood is a special and fanciful land where the possibilities for adventure are endless. It is into this place that Catherine Marshall takes us, a world where frogs learn lessons of humility, kings learn to be kings, and two little girls help us to see ourselves a little more clearly.

Catherine Marshall LeSourd early developed a love for children's books. Her parents read her bedtime stories and she always begged for more, delighted with the antics of mischievous kittens or raccoons. Years later when Catherine had a son of her own, she continued the family tradition of reading at bedtime.

Catherine became one of America's most beloved inspirational authors, and her twenty books have sold more than 18 million copies. But she never forgot her early love of children's books. Among her publications were two books for young people containing the favorite stories and prayers of the Marshall family: *Friends with God* and *God Loves You.*

About the time Catherine's grandchildren were discovering the wonders of books, she wrote the text for the beautiful volume *Catherine Marshall's Story Bible,* which includes 80 full-color illustrations by children from around the world. She wanted children to hear about God's ways with His people, she said, and to see "the glorious difference Jesus Christ had made in the lives of so many."

After Catherine's death in 1983, I was going through her files when I came across a thick folder marked "Possibles for a Children's Book." The first item typed on yellowed carbon paper was entitled "The Dog Who Had an Idea." There was more—verses of Scripture, notes she had scribbled, and a collection of her favorite children's poems by noted authors.

Here, unquestionably, was Catherine's planned fourth children's book, a fanciful book of people and animals and foreign lands, a book in which every story, like a fable, taught a particular truth or lesson as the characters made discoveries in the world around them.

Two other people have lent their expertise to this book. David Hazard, author of the children's book *The Peaceable Kingdom,* worked with Catherine on the *Story Bible.* It was natural for him to select and edit material from Catherine's files for this volume. One of his own poems has been included because Catherine was so taken with it. And Joe Boddy, a gifted artist, has created the beautiful full-color illustrations for this volume, capturing the warmth and whimsy of the stories. Joe has illustrated more than thirty children's books, among them the *Mr. T and Me* series and *Abram, Abram, Where Are We Going?* for which he won a 1984 C. S. Lewis citation.

We trust that this book will touch many; certainly children will delight in the magic of these pages. But we think adults will find a treasure here, too—adults who, like Catherine, have never quite let go of the special joys and wonders of childhood.

—Leonard E. LeSourd
Evergreen Farm, Virginia

For a Spring Day

Adapted from Song of Solomon 2:11-13

Look! Look in the yard and in the meadow,
the cold, gray rainclouds have blown away.
Flowers are bursting in the fresh green woods.
The season of singing is here!

Just listen!
The bright, clear song of the dove
rings from the top of the evergreen tree.
While back in the orchard, the silent blossoms
creep in pink and white parade up the vines,
and smell so sweet on the morning breeze.

Come! The Lord, our friend, is calling!
Come on, let's venture into His world!

The Dog Who Had an Idea

Marcus was a big brown and white dog. He had dark patches around both eyes, white paws, and a great round tummy—for Marcus weighed more than 300 pounds! He was a good dog except for one thing. Marcus was lazy.

Every morning, the little boy who owned Marcus leaped out of bed excitedly. His name was Bobby, and he loved to be outdoors. After breakfast Bobby looked out across the warm, sunshiny fields and called, "Come on, Marcus! Let's go out and have some fun!"

Then Marcus would have to follow.

But he did not like to run, or wade through the brook, or fetch the sticks that Bobby threw. He always wished he were home, sleeping on his mat by the door.

One morning Marcus woke up with a new idea. It was the first idea that had ever crossed his doggy mind. He thought, *I'll pretend that I can't hear. And when Bobby calls me out to play, I'll lie very still with my eyes shut. Then he'll go away—and I can stay home and sleep!*

And sure enough, right after Bobby took his breakfast plate to the sink, he patted Marcus on the head. "Come on, boy. Let's go!"

But Marcus just lay there by the kitchen door with his eyes shut tight.

Bobby bent down and patted his head. "Marcus—? Did you hear me?"

Marcus looked up at him, but did not move one paw.

"Marcus! *Are you coming?*" Bobby shouted.

And still the big dog did not budge. He looked at Bobby as if to ask, "What did you say?"

Bobby's mother had come to see what the noise was about, and Bobby told her, "I think something is wrong with his ears. Marcus just can't hear me anymore." And off he went to play alone.

But that evening at suppertime, Bobby's mother was slicing a delicious roast for supper. One small slice of meat slipped from her fingers. Even though Marcus was at the other end of the house—a hallway and four rooms away—he heard the meat land *kersplat!* on the floor.

He came galloping into the kitchen, with a flurry of furry paws, and gobbled down the bit of meat. When Bobby's mother saw this, she knew Marcus was only pretending he couldn't hear. And after supper that night, she whispered a plan in Bobby's ear.

The next morning Marcus lay on his mat by the door with his eyes shut tight. Bobby ate his breakfast as usual—but something was wrong. Bobby wasn't whistling as he usually

did. Or slurping his orange juice as usual. Marcus peeked with one eye, and he was frightened.

Bobby and his mother were moving their lips, just as if they were talking to one another—but no sound was coming out!

And it was the same the next day, and the next, and the day after that. Marcus felt awful. In his doggy mind he thought, *Oh no! I really have lost my hearing.*

The very next morning—on a billowy, wind-washed day— Bobby came down to breakfast and shouted, "Come on, Marcus! Dad bought me a new kite. Let's go out and see how high she flies!"

Marcus was so happy to hear Bobby's voice that he leaped to his feet. "Woof!" he said. Which meant, "Let's go!"

And as Marcus bounced across the yard, chasing at Bobby's heels, a new idea came into his doggy mind: *Lying just doesn't pay. Even acting a lie can get you in trouble.*

And Marcus was never lazy again.

Look for a Lovely Thing

"Night" by Sara Teasdale

Stars over snow,
and in the west a planet
swings below a star—

Look for a lovely thing
and you will find it.
It is not far.
It will never be far.

The King Who Burned the Biscuits

The days were dark and troubled when King Alfred took the throne of England a long, long time ago. Rough men, called Vikings, had come to England. With spear and sword they rode through the countryside, until they had conquered almost every town.

Finally there was only one small town left, a poor village surrounded by a thick forest, that the Vikings had not yet captured. There King Alfred and his men hid themselves.

Now Alfred, though a king, was still a very young man. He had not had time to travel around England much; most of the English people had never seen him before. And so it was that when Alfred came to the small village, no one recognized him as their king.

Tying his horse to a tree beside the hut of a poor shepherd, Alfred tapped at the door. The shepherd's wife opened the door timidly and said, "Who are you? And what do you want?"

The king could not let the woman know who he really was. So he replied, "I am only a wayfarer. I need a place to spend the night. I have no money to pay you, but I can work for my supper."

The woman looked at Alfred's good face and let him come inside the hut. There the king saw a cheerful blaze dancing in the fireplace and smelled the aroma of hot biscuits baking.

The woman pointed to a pan at the edge of the fire. "I have to go out to the fields to call my husband in for supper. But I've just put these biscuits on to bake. You can earn your supper by watching them. Mind you, keep a good eye on them and don't let them burn." And without another word, she hurried out.

Carefully Alfred lifted the lid of the pan. The biscuits were just turning a light, golden brown. *Hmm*, he thought, *I wonder how I'll know when they are done*. You see, since Alfred was a king, he had never in his life had to bake biscuits.

And so he sat down by the fire and waited. And while he waited, he thought about how he and his men could drive the Vikings out of their land. He wondered if they could really do it. After all, the Vikings were powerful, and Alfred's men were not good fighters. How could they ever win England back? Should they just give up?

Alfred was muddling through these unhappy thoughts when—oh no! He smelled something burning! Lifting the pan lid, he saw that the supper biscuits had burned and shriveled into hard black crusts.

Just as he was lifting the smoking pan from the fire, the shepherd and his wife came home. When they saw what Alfred had done, they were furious.

16

"Now we shall go hungry tonight," wailed the woman.
"Yes," growled the shepherd, "and all because of a foolish young man who doesn't even know how to watch biscuits. What good are you? You're worthless. You'll never amount to anything."

That night, when Alfred curled up on his straw mat to sleep, he was hungry and lonely. The shepherd and his wife had gone to bed without saying another word to him. It was a very dark moment in Alfred's young life.

But when he closed his eyes, he remembered his gold crown with its red rubies, green emeralds, and sparkling blue topaz. He was not worthless, no matter what the shepherd had said. Even if invaders conquered his land. Even if his troops were not strong. Even if he didn't know how to bake biscuits! A warm good feeling touched his heart, and he fell into a peaceful sleep. After all, *he was a king!*

Not long afterwards, Alfred and his men struck out through the forest against the Vikings. Everyone was surprised at how bravely they fought. Soon the Vikings were driven out of England. Alfred went back to his throne. He built schools and libraries and ships and churches. He had the Bible translated into Anglo-Saxon, which was the language the common people spoke in those days.

One day Alfred sent messengers to bring the shepherd and his wife to him. When the poor couple saw Alfred the king seated on his splendid throne, they fell on their knees, terrified. It was their king they had scolded. They'd even called him worthless!

But Alfred said, "Get up. You have no need to fear. I've brought you here to reward you, for in your hut I learned a great lesson.

"A young person should not be discouraged if there are some things he cannot do well. Each one of us must find the things he can do best. And then he must do them with joy and a grateful heart."

Each of us can be like Alfred. There may be things we cannot do well at all. But some things we can do very well. Alfred could not bake biscuits, yet he became one of England's greatest kings.

God's Little Nightlights

"Firefly" by Elizabeth Madox Roberts

A little light is going by,
Is going up to see the sky,
A little light with wings.

I never could have thought of it,
to have a little bug all lit
And made to go on wings!

The Boy on the Fence

One sunny afternoon a man was walking to the post office to get his mail. He was strolling by a playground when he saw the strangest thing.

A group of boys and girls were playing soccer. One team wore blue shirts and the other wore red shirts. They raced from one end of the field to the other, laughing and booting the ball, having the best time.

The strange thing was this: A tall fence stood beside the playing field, and perched on top of it, like a bird, was a boy.

The man was curious, and he walked toward the fence. As he got closer, he could see that the boy was watching the soccer match eagerly. The team with the blue shirts kicked the white-and-black ball up the field, and the boy cheered and hollered. With one powerful kick, the ball sailed into the goal.

For a moment, it seemed that the boy was going to jump down from the fence and join in the game. But the red-shirt team was already kicking the ball up the field. In short order, they had scored a goal, too.

The boy did not get down after all. He stayed right where he was, perched atop the fence.

The man was right beneath him by then, and he called out, "Say, you must have quite a good view of the game from up there."

"Oh, yes," the boy sighed. He sounded a little gloomy.

The man felt sorry for him. "Won't they let you play?" he asked.

"Sure, they'll let me play," the boy responded. "I'm pretty good at soccer. They'd let me play in a minute if...."

"If what?" the man asked.

"If I could only decide *which* team I want to be on," he explained. "Just when it looks like the blue team is winning, the red team makes a goal. Right now the score is tied, and I want to be on the winning team."

The man looked at the boy's face. It looked like something was hurting him. "It must not be very comfortable sitting on that fence," the man commented.

"It's not," replied the boy. "In fact, I'm starting to get a little sore."

Then the boy turned to watch the soccer game. And the man continued his walk to the post office.

A little while later, the man was walking home past the playground. The game had finished and everyone had gone home. Almost everyone.

There was the boy. He had finally climbed down from the fence, and he scuffed along the sidewalk unhappily with his head hung down.

"What happened?" asked the man when they were side by side.

"I finally made up my mind which side I wanted to be on, but by then the game was over. I never even got to play."

"I'm sorry," said the man. "Perhaps you have learned something today. You have to get on one side or the other; you have to choose. That's when you are free to have fun."

And that's the way it is for us when we choose to live as God wants us to. Then we are on His side. And we can never lose when we choose to do the things God tells us to do.

Let's Play

*Adapted from
the book of Isaiah*

When you go out,
Go out with joy!
March like a band,
Play the music of peace!

Then the mountains and hills
Will burst into singing
And all the trees of the field
will clap their hands!

Scary Things Around the Corner

It was a hot summer day. Jill skipped along the city sidewalk on her way home from the store. Her mother had given her money to buy a quart of milk and some bread, which she carried in a brown paper bag.

In her pocket—jingling and jangling—were silver coins, the change the grocer had pressed into her hand. Her mother had said the leftover money was all hers to spend!

Jill had looked over all the good things at the grocery store, but did not see anything she liked. So she had slipped the extra money into her pocket, hoping to find just the right treat on her way home.

Out on the busy sidewalk, she skipped along. The pavement was hot, and as she went along quickly, the coins jingled happily in her pocket. Until a gloomy thought crossed her mind.

What if the coins bounce right out of my pocket? she thought. At once she stopped skipping. Instead she kept her

eyes on the sidewalk, watching for loose stones that might make her trip.

Now Jill trudged along beside the tall brick buildings. She grew hot and uncomfortable. But still she wondered what sort of special treat she would buy with her money. Maybe a cold vanilla ice cream cone with chocolate sprinkles!

Jill had been walking beside an old storefront, and was about to round the corner. She froze. A new fearful thought came to her: *What if someone is hiding around that corner? Like a robber!*

To make things worse, at that very moment she heard a mysterious sound—a rumbly sort of noise.

Clutching her brown bag tightly, Jill did not wait to see what it was. She was so frightened that she ran as fast as she could, past the corner of the building and across the street. She caught only a glimpse of the man who was coming around the corner toward her—and she did not even look back to see who it was.

When she was out of sight, the ice cream man stopped pushing his rumbly old cart, and scratched his head. "That little girl looked pretty hot and tired," he said to himself. "I'll bet she would have enjoyed eating one of my ice cream cones. I wonder what scared her."

Some people are just like the little girl in this story. They are always worried about what will happen tomorrow. Or next week. They are afraid that something bad is waiting just around the corner.

But the truth is, there are mostly good things waiting for us around the corner. We can spoil all the fun if we are always afraid of what *might* happen.

As Jesus has said: "Don't be afraid—and don't let your heart be troubled. Trust Me!"

Under God's Canopy

(by David Hazard)

Under God's canopy of soft night sky
the world's eyes are drowsy and the stars wheel by
as Mother fluffs the pillow for my sleepy head
and Father whispers prayers with me—now, into bed!

Rings of winging angels guide me in my dreams
in a peaceful land of golden fields and singing streams,
where flowers push away the thorns, the crooked path unbends,
the lion and the lamb curl up in peace as friends.

Where nations lay their guns aside, no blood is shed,
the poor are rich, the sick are whole, the hungry fed,
and children wake to find the sun is sweeping high
under God's canopy of bright new sky.

The Frog Who Flew
("I Did It")

At the edge of a pond, hidden among the reeds and cattails, there lived a boastful frog.

On a flat rock, he warmed his green back in the sun all day. Throughout the summer, he dozed by day, dreaming about how great and important he was. Really, he did nothing but sit on his rock and eat and sleep. But at night, when the moon shone on the dark water and the breeze whispered in the reeds, he opened his bulging black eyes. Then he would croak out loud, *"I-did-it! I-did-it!"*

Summer passed, and one fall evening a flock of brown and gray geese landed in the pond. They paddled 'round and 'round the shining surface of the water. They had stopped for a rest on their way from the cold north to the sunny south for the winter.

And that night, the frog sat croaking loudly as usual. A slippery silver-colored fish swished into the shallow water at the pond's edge. He slipped his head above the surface and asked, "What's all the noise about?"

"I-did-it! I-did-it!" croaked the frog.

"What did you do?"

"All sorts of things," the frog replied. "In fact, I can do anything I want to do."

The fish peered at him with one silver saucer eye. *"Anything?* You say you can do anything?"

"That's right," said the frog, and his wide froggy mouth turned up in a huge smile.

The fish thought for a moment, and as he thought, he watched the brown and gray geese paddling about the pond. Then he smiled to himself, for he was certain he had thought up something the frog could never do. "Well, Frog," said the fish, "can you fly?"

"Fly? Why that's as simple as anything. Of course I can fly," he boasted. "You just come around tomorrow morning and you'll see."

Now that frog *was* clever. From the moment the fish swished away beneath the water, he began to think of a plan.

At dawn the next day, just as the sun peeked through the blankets of morning mist, the geese began to honk noisily. They stretched their wings like banners and beat the cold air, preparing for their flight. Two boys from a nearby farm heard the honking, and stood watching from a hill overlooking the pond.

The fish slid his head up out of the water. He had brought along all his friends to see what the frog would do. He said to the frog, "Well, it looks like quite a big crowd has come to watch you fly. Now let's see you do it."

The frog did not reply. A goose was paddling by his rock, and the frog said to him, "Excuse me, friend. I wonder if you can pull up one of these long, stiff reeds?"

"Certainly," said the goose. He gripped a reed in his bill, and pulled and pulled until it was free.

Then the frog called to a second goose, "Please take the other end of this reed in your bill."

Now the two geese were holding the reed between them, one at each end. "Now I'll take hold of the middle," said the frog, "and you can carry me away with you."

With that, he seized the middle of the reed in his mouth. The geese beat their wings, and the fish watched in amazement as the frog sailed up into the morning sky, dangling from the reed.

The two farm boys watching from the hill saw the wonderful sight. One of them shouted, "What a great idea! Who could have thought of such a thing? What smart geese!"

Far up in the air, still gripping the reed in his mouth, the frog heard the boy's shouts. Why, the boys were giving credit to the geese for *his* bright idea. And this was more than the boastful frog could stand.

Without thinking, he shouted back, "I-did-it! I-did-it!" And, of course, the moment he opened his mouth to call, he let go of the reed. In terror, he fell down and down and down.

Fortunately, the geese had been circling over the pond.

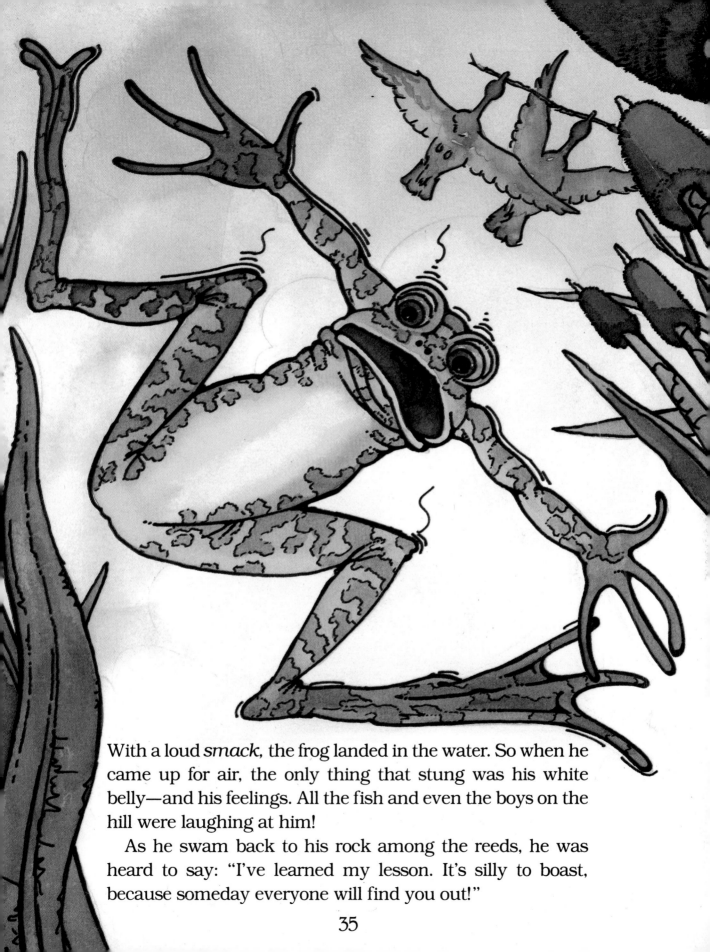

With a loud *smack,* the frog landed in the water. So when he came up for air, the only thing that stung was his white belly—and his feelings. All the fish and even the boys on the hill were laughing at him!

As he swam back to his rock among the reeds, he was heard to say: "I've learned my lesson. It's silly to boast, because someday everyone will find you out!"

Do You Know Who Made You?

(Adapted from "The Lamb"
by William Blake)

Little lamb, who made you?
Do you know who made you?
Gave you life and bid you feed
By the stream and o'er the meadow;
Gave you clothing of delight
softest clothing, woolly, bright;
gave you such a tender voice,
making all the fields rejoice?

Little lamb, who made you?
Do you know who made you?
Little lamb, I'll tell you!
He is called by your name,
for He calls *Himself* a lamb!
He is meek, and He is mild;
He became a little child.
I a child, and you a lamb,
we are called by His name.

Little lamb, God bless you!

A Blackbird Never Forgets

After school one day, a little girl named Peggy was busy doing her homework. She sat at the desk by the window in her room and worked quickly. She wanted to finish so she could go outside and play before supper.

As she was just adding up her last arithmetic problem, she heard a *thump* at her window. Looking out, Peggy saw only the swingset in the yard. Then she noticed her cat, prowling by the border of flowers just beneath her window. But wait!

Lying in the flowerbed was a young blackbird with a twisted wing. It must have flown into the window by accident. It lay there stunned, unable to fly or hop. And Peggy's cat was about to pounce on it!

Peggy pulled open the window. "Scat!" she shouted. And not a moment too soon. Her cat was startled—and disappointed at losing its snack. Twitching its tail in a sulk, the cat turned and walked away.

Quickly Peggy hurried outside and scooped up the wounded blackbird. She brought him into her room, where she emptied an old shoebox of doll clothes she'd been saving. She lined the box with soft tissues, and gently set the bird inside. Instead of going out to play with her friends, she stayed indoors and nursed her patient.

"You'll be all right in there," Peggy said softly. "When you're better, I'll let you fly away." The blackbird only cocked his head and looked at her with great curiosity.

That evening Peggy saved some bread from her supper and took it in to the bird. At first he would not eat. But in a little while he began to peck at the bread, until it was all gone.

"I'll get some more for you," Peggy reassured him.

So it went for two or three days. Every free moment Peggy spent with the blackbird. Once she even sang him a song she had learned in school, though it made her feel a little silly singing to a bird. Still, the bird did not seem to mind.

And one afternoon, when Peggy rushed into her room after school, she noticed that her window was open a little. The blackbird was gone. Her mother had dusted that day, and she had opened the window to let in a little fresh air.

Peggy sat on her bed feeling gloomy. She knew that the bird's wing must have gotten stronger; otherwise he would not have been able to fly away. Still, she felt sorry that she had not had the chance to say goodbye.

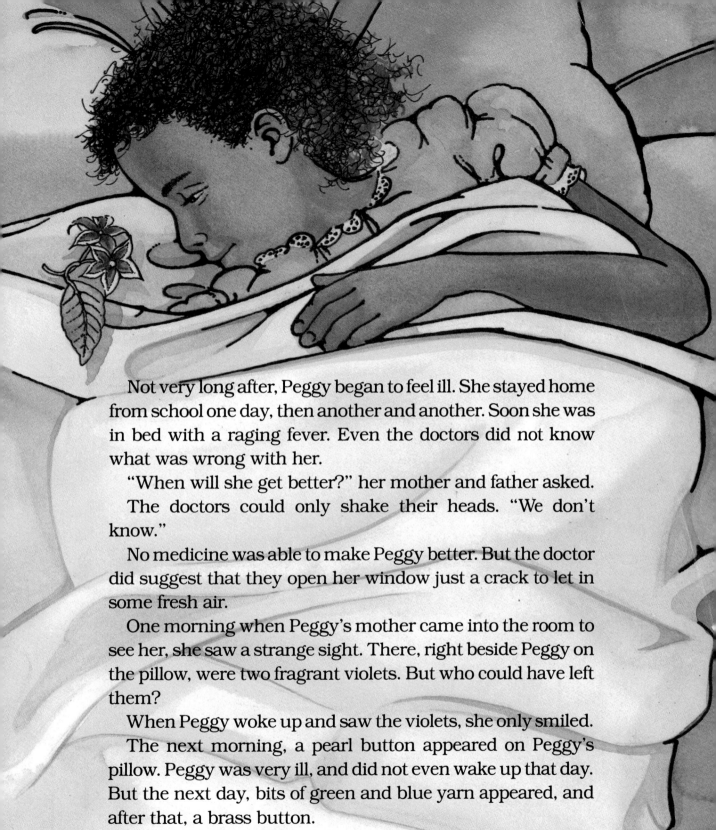

Not very long after, Peggy began to feel ill. She stayed home from school one day, then another and another. Soon she was in bed with a raging fever. Even the doctors did not know what was wrong with her.

"When will she get better?" her mother and father asked.

The doctors could only shake their heads. "We don't know."

No medicine was able to make Peggy better. But the doctor did suggest that they open her window just a crack to let in some fresh air.

One morning when Peggy's mother came into the room to see her, she saw a strange sight. There, right beside Peggy on the pillow, were two fragrant violets. But who could have left them?

When Peggy woke up and saw the violets, she only smiled.

The next morning, a pearl button appeared on Peggy's pillow. Peggy was very ill, and did not even wake up that day. But the next day, bits of green and blue yarn appeared, and after that, a brass button.

Peggy's mother was puzzled by the mysterious objects that seemed to come from nowhere. It all remained a mystery, until one afternoon.

While Peggy was napping, her mother slipped quietly into her room. She went over to the window and was about to close it when she saw the most curious thing. On the sill sat a blackbird with his head cocked to one side. Before the mother could *shoo* him away and close the window, he began to sing. As he sang, other birds lighted on the sill one by one—until the sill was crowded with birds and Peggy's room was flooded with song!

By then Peggy was awake. She even sat up in bed for the first time in days and listened to the bird chorus. Peggy's father came in to join her mother, and they smiled at the

feathered singers, who whistled and warbled away.

From that day on, Peggy grew stronger and stronger. And after a time, the doctors said she was healthy again.

Although the doctors could not explain what made Peggy better, she and her parents knew. Because she had given her love to a small friend in need, the little bird had not forgotten her. His song of joy had touched her heart and helped to heal her body.

And so Peggy learned that even the smallest act of kindness is never forgotten.

My Pocket

I carry around in my pocket
my secret and wonderful things—
rocks, gumballs, a balloon,
an old penny, a spoon,
and a ball made of all-colored strings.

And I love my small pocket, you see—
no one knows what is in it, but me!

Now my head is just like a pocket,
with thoughts that I tuck there inside,
secrets kept from my brother,
things I don't tell my mother—
what a good place for those thoughts to hide!

But a head's not so dark, or so small
that *God* can't see in it—secrets and all.

Thorns and Roses

In Germany, they tell a story about two little sisters who lived beside a rustling and mysterious forest.

One hot and lazy summer day, the girls were playing in the cool shade at the forest's edge when they discovered a path. It was mossy and overgrown with tangled roots, and it seemed to beckon them in under the shadowy trees.

Quickly they dashed off to find their mother. "Please," they begged when they found her. "Can we see what the path leads to?"

The mother's eyes sparkled. "Yes," she replied in a hushed voice. "That will be a wonderful adventure!"

And so the girls dashed to the head of the path. Carefully they picked their way through tangled thickets and briars, across a splashing brook, until the path ended. And what did they find?

At the heart of the forest was an old abandoned garden. Someone had planted it many years before, but now it had gone wild. Pink foxgloves bobbed like bells. Yellow daisies ran wild along the path. Purple turtleheads and the white star of the eidelweiss flower nodded in the stirring air.

Most beautiful of all were the enormous rosebushes. Their branches hung like waterfalls of red, white, and yellow blooms.

The two girls caught their breath at such loveliness. And before they thought, each girl reached out a hand to pick a rose—and each pricked her finger on a thorn hidden beneath the leaves and petals.

Back at home, the girls' mother waited eagerly for them to return from their forest adventure. It wasn't long before she heard singing coming from inside the woods—but only one girl's voice brought the sweet melody. What had happened to her other girl?

Concerned, the mother ran outside. Coming from the forest path, she saw the other girl with a frown on her face. She ran to her mother's arms, and hugged her as tears of disappointment rolled down her cheeks.

"Oh, Mother," she wept, holding forth her pricked finger, "we found nothing but thorns."

As the mother comforted her, the other child came skipping from the forest. In her arms was a sweet-smelling bouquet, like a cloud of red, white, and yellow. She handed her mother the roses and said happily, "We found the most beautiful spot on earth. It was like heaven—roses, roses everywhere."

Those two little girls are like many people. Some find thorns in everything they do. As a result they are always disappointed and full of complaints. Yet others see the bright and beautiful side of things. They are always looking for "roses, roses everywhere."

And when you look for roses, you always find them.

Which sort of person are you?

Thank You, Lord

Dear Lord,
   Thank You for rain
   that dimples the puddles,
   sings in the drain,
   drenches the garden,
   taps on the pane.
   Thank You for quiet
   cloud-washed days.
   Thank You, Lord, for rain!
         Amen

Dear Lord,
   I know the sun gets up
   and sweeps the sky
   and lights the world
   so I can play.

But tell me, Lord,
   if I hop out of bed
   early enough,
   will I catch a peek
   of You
   as You start the day?
         Amen

Dear Lord,
Thank You for the quiet snow.
Thank You for the winds that blow.
They dress the trees in lacy ice.

Thank You for my snug, small bed,
and for the pillow 'neath my head.
Winter is pretty; and keeping warm feels nice!
                                        Amen

Good-Night

(by Victor Hugo)

Good-night! Good-night!
Far flies the light;
But still God's love
Shall flame above,
Making all bright,
Good-night! Good-night!

48